MW00915657

DIAL BOOKS FOR YOUNG READERS

A division of Penguin Young Readers Group • Published by The
Penguin Group • Penguin Group (USA) Inc., 375 Hudson Street, New York,
NY 10014, U.S.A. • Penguin Group (Canada), 90 Eglinton Avenue East, Suite
700, Toronto, Ontario, Canada M4P 2Y3 (a division of Pearson Penguin Canada
Inc.) • Penguin Books Ltd, 80 Strand, London WC2R 0RL, England • Penguin Ireland, 25
St. Stephen's Green, Dublin 2, Ireland (a division of Penguin Books Ltd) • Penguin Group
(Australia), 250 Camberwell Road, Camberwell, Victoria 3124, Australia (a division of Pearson
Australia Group Pty Ltd) • Penguin Books India Pvt Ltd, 11 Community Centre, Panchsheel Park,
New Delhi - 110 017, India • Penguin Group (NZ), 67 Apollo Drive, Rosedale, Auckland 0632, New
Zealand (a division of Pearson New Zealand Ltd) • Penguin Books (South Africa) (Pty) Ltd, 24 Sturdee
Avenue, Rosebank, Johannesburg 2196, South Africa • Penguin Books Ltd, Registered Offices: 80 Strand,
London WC2R 0RL, England

Text copyright © 2013 by Randall de Sève • Illustrations copyright © 2013 by Paul Schmid
All rights reserved. No part of this book may be reproduced, scanned, or distributed in any printed or
electronic form without permission. Please do not participate in or encourage piracy of copyrighted
materials in violation of the author's rights. Purchase only authorized editions.

The publisher does not have any control over and does not assume any responsibility for author or third
party websites or their content.

Designed by Mina Chung • Text set in Metallophile Sp8 • Manufactured in China on acid-free paper

10 9 8 7 6 5 4 3 2 1

Library of Congress Cataloging-in-Publication Data

De Sève, Randall.
Peanut and Fifi have a ball / by Randall de Sève ; illustrations by Paul Schmid.   p. cm.
Summary: Squabbling over a toy ball, two sisters ultimately learn that playing together is even more fun.
ISBN 978-0-8037-3578-1 (hardcover)
[1. Balls (Sporting goods)—Fiction. 2. Sharing—Fiction. 3. Sisters—Fiction.] I. Schmid, Paul, ill. II. Title.
PZ7.D4504Pe 2013   [E]—dc23   2012014355

This art was created digitally.

ALWAYS LEARNING   PEARSON

To Paulina and Fia, of course!
—R.d.S.

For Mom and Dad
—P.S.

Peanut & Fifi have a ball

by
Randall de Sève

illustrations by
Paul Schmid

 Dial Books for Young Readers

an imprint of Penguin Group (USA) Inc.

Peanut had a ball.

It was brand-new.

It was bright blue.

And it was special.

Fifi wanted to play with it.

So she tried grabbing.

But that didn't work.

So she tried politeness:

"Pleeeeeaaaase."

But Peanut didn't want to share.

Her ball was new.

And it was special.

Still, Fifi wanted to
play with it.

"Basketball?"

But Peanut just hugged
her ball tighter.

Still, Fifi wanted to
play with it.

So she made the ball a hat.
"It has flowers and a live bird on top!"

"My ball doesn't need a hat,"
Peanut said.

Still, Fifi wouldn't give up.

She put on a sparkly cape
and glued a silver star to
her forehead.
"Where is my crystal ball?"
she asked in a funny voice.

"Not here," said Peanut.

"Check the closet."

Fifi came back wearing a chef's hat.

"Dough!

It's bread dough

and we're bakers

and we've got to knead it

and pound it

and push it . . ."

"Not dough,"

Peanut replied.

"Just a ball."

But Fifi thought more of it than that.

So she sent the ball a note:

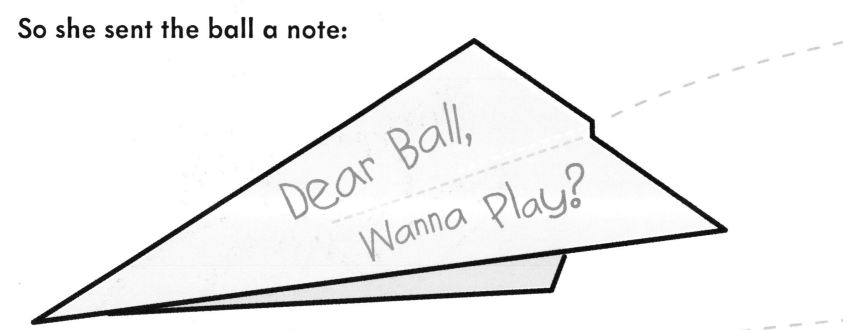

A note came back:

So Fifi went away.

But then she returned . . .

with a seal!

"His name is Bob.
We can teach him tricks
and join the circus
and travel all over the world!

"And look, I packed our bags.
We have a change of clothes
and pajamas
and our toothbrushes
and sandwiches
and a book for you
and a book for me . . .

and lots of fish for Bob."

"Okay!"

"No thanks," said Fifi.

She was on to something new.
(Something blue!)

And having a ball.

The end.

(or not . . .)

"Hey Fifi, check out this cool planet!"

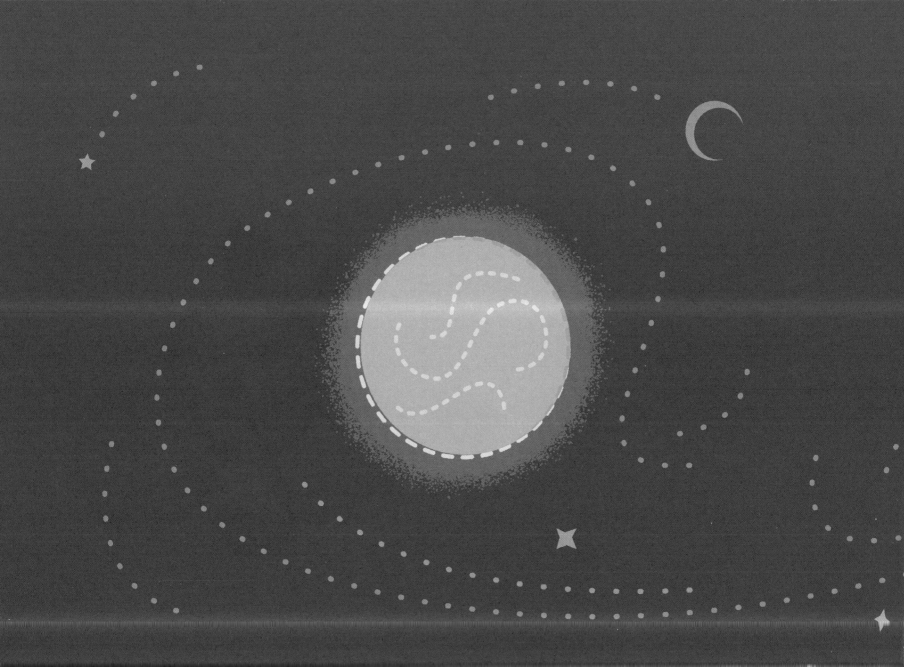